Murphy, Murphy, Murphy Marguerite,
I wrote a book
just for you,
because you are so sweet!
—M.S.

To Roberta, Richard, Laraine, and Paul,
all with excellent egg-counting skills
—M.F.

Text copyright © 2014 by Marilyn Sadler
Cover art and interior illustrations copyright © 2014 by Michael Fleming

Visit us on the Web!
randomhouse.com/kids

Educators and librarians, for a variety of teaching tools, visit us at
RHTeachersLibrarians.com

Library of Congress Cataloging-in-Publication Data
Sadler, Marilyn.
Ten eggs in a nest / by Marilyn Sadler ; illustrated by Michael Fleming. — First edition.
  pages cm. — (A bright and early book ; [BE40])
Summary: Red is so excited that Gwen has laid a nest full of eggs, he rushes out to buy a worm to feed each of the increasing number of chicks as they hatch.
ISBN 978-0-449-81082-8 (trade) — ISBN 978-0-375-97151-8 (lib. bdg.) —
ISBN 978-0-375-98139-5 (ebook)
[1. Chickens—Fiction. 2. Eggs—Fiction. 3. Counting.] I. Fleming, Michael, illustrator.
II. Title.
PZ7.S1239Ten 2014 [E]—dc23 2012051234

Printed in the United States of America

10 9 8 7 6 5 4 3 2 1

First Edition

Ten Eggs in a Nest

By Marilyn Sadler
Illustrated by Michael Fleming

A Bright and Early Book
From BEGINNER BOOKS®
A Division of Random House, Inc.

Gwen the hen
had laid all her eggs.
She was very excited.
She was going to be
a mother!

Red Rooster was excited too.
He was going to be a father!

"How many eggs
did you lay today?"
Red asked Gwen
as he tried to peek
into her nest.

"Puck-puck!" Gwen clucked.
"It's bad luck
to count your eggs
before they hatch."

Red did not want Gwen
to have bad luck.
So he did not count her eggs.
He made her
a grass salad instead.

Gwen was eating her salad.
Then she got a big surprise.
One of her eggs hatched!
It was ONE beautiful
baby chick.

"I will go to the market," said Red, "to buy our new baby ONE worm!"

Red strutted into
Worm World.
He held his head high.
He puffed his chest out.
Pinky Pig
was behind the counter.

"I have ONE new baby chick!"
said Red.
Pinky was happy for Red.
It could not have happened
to a nicer rooster.

"This one's on me," said Pinky
as he dropped ONE worm
into Red's bag.

Red could not wait
to feed the worm
to his new baby chick.

But when Red got home,
Gwen had a surprise for him!
TWO more baby chicks
had hatched!

"ONE plus TWO makes THREE baby chicks!" said Gwen. ONE! TWO! THREE!

"You could knock me over with a feather," said Red.

Red gave Gwen ONE worm
and then hurried back
to Worm World.

"I need TWO more worms!"
Red told Pinky.

"ONE! TWO!" counted Pinky as he dropped TWO worms into Red's bag.

"ONE! TWO!" counted Red
as he dropped TWO coins
into Pinky's pocket.

Red could not wait
to feed the worms
to his new baby chicks.

But when Red got home,
Gwen had a big surprise
for him!
THREE more baby chicks
had hatched!

"ONE plus TWO plus THREE makes SIX baby chicks!" said Gwen.

ONE! TWO! THREE!
FOUR! FIVE! SIX!
"Oh, dear," said Red.
"Oh, yes," said Gwen.
Red gave Gwen TWO worms
and then hurried back
to Worm World.

"I need THREE more worms!"
Red told Pinky.

"ONE! TWO! THREE!"
counted Pinky
as he dropped THREE worms
into Red's bag.

"ONE! TWO! THREE!"
counted Red
as he dropped THREE coins
into Pinky's pocket.

Red could not wait
to feed the worms
to his new baby chicks.

But when he got home,
Gwen had a great big
surprise for him!
FOUR more baby chicks
had hatched!

"ONE plus TWO plus
THREE plus FOUR more
makes TEN baby chicks!"
clucked Gwen.

ONE! TWO! THREE!
FOUR! FIVE! SIX!
SEVEN! EIGHT!
NINE! TEN!

Red was speechless.
You could have
knocked him over
with a feather.

Red gave Gwen
THREE worms
and then hurried
back to Worm World.

Pinky had FOUR worms
ready for Red when he flew
through the door.

"ONE! TWO! THREE! FOUR!"
counted Pinky
as he dropped FOUR worms
into Red's bag.
"ONE! TWO! THREE! FOUR!"
counted Red
as he dropped FOUR coins
into Pinky's pocket.

Red could not wait
to feed the worms
to his new baby chicks.

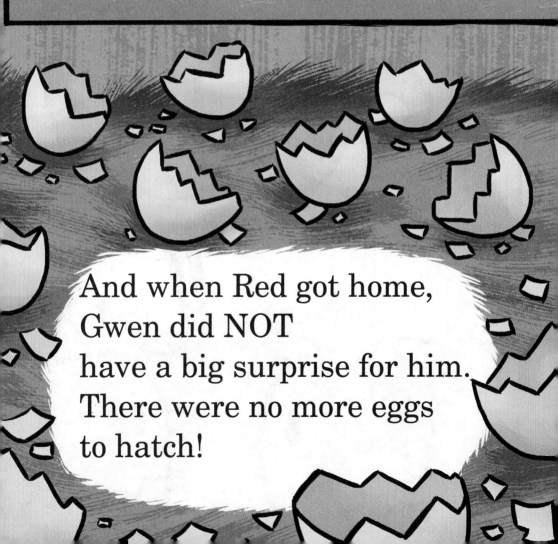

And when Red got home,
Gwen did NOT
have a big surprise for him.
There were no more eggs
to hatch!

Finally, Red got to feed
his new baby chicks.
He fed them each ONE worm.

ONE! TWO! THREE!
FOUR! FIVE! SIX!
SEVEN! EIGHT!
NINE! TEN!
"We have TEN new
baby chicks
in our nest," said Red.

Gwen was happy for Red.
It could not have happened
to a nicer rooster.

"This one's on me," said Gwen
as she planted ONE peck
on Red's cheek!

BRIGHT and EARLY BOOKS for BEGINNING Beginners